OATMEAL

By: PATTI LETTS

DEDICATED TO:

VETERANS SERENDIPITY RANCH
AND
LIGHTHOUSE BODY OF CHRIST CHURCH.

To Debbie Praay and Marilyn Bowen, Directors of Veterans Serendipity Ranch
Equine Therapy program; to Jerry & Josette Kloha, owners of the ranch; who very generously offered free use of
their facility for Veterans Serendipity Ranch. Also a very heartfelt thanks to my editor, Deb, who worked like a
"horse" to finish the job.

My name is…well, I guess I don't have a people name yet. I live on a farm with lots of other ponies. Sometimes the man that feeds us calls us minis, but my dam (that's what they call horses that are Moms) says mini isn't a name, it's what we are.

I am a 3 year old miniature horse. We are very, very little horses. Smaller than Shetland ponies, or welsh ponies or even some big dogs, like Great Danes!

The man who feeds us is Mac. People who visit the farm call him Mini-Mac. When visitors come to the farm, Mac brings some of us from the barn or pasture so they can look at us. Sometimes the people bring trailers with them.

That's when we know one or two of us are going to a new home. One day a man and woman came to visit. Their name was Anderson. They brought their son with them. He was skinny and pale, and he wore a funny helmet that wasn't a riding helmet. They told

Mac that they had a farm where they stabled other peoples' horses. When their boy wandered towards the barn, they told Mac that their son, Andrew, had epilepsy. That was why he wore the helmet. It was for protection when he had seizures. Even with the medicine he took, he could still have one. That's why he had to sit by, watching his friends (those that boarded their horses at his parents' stable) ride off without him.

And having his parents walk beside him on a horse, made him feel like a baby. But Mr. and Mrs. Anderson had come up with an idea. They told Mac about it. "It's worth trying" he said, so they talked with Mac awhile longer.

Then he led several of us from the pasture into a smaller pen so the boy and his parents could get a good look at us. Mac let them come into the pen.

The other minis were nervous about the boy with the helmet and wouldn't come near him. I was curious about him, though, and stood still as he came closer. A slight breeze blew his smell to me. Oh, my, WHAT was that wonderful smell?

I had to find out. I knew it was coming from the boy,

so I met him halfway across the pen while his parents watched. The smell got more mouth-watering the closer I got to him. I sniffed him carefully while he patted me. I sniffed his face. No delicious smell there, just boy smell.

Then I sniffed his feet. Definitely NOT the feet!

Raising my head to his pocket, and SCORE!

Something round and melt in my mouth yummy. Andrew laughed when my muzzle came out of his pocket chewing happily. "I think he likes your oatmeal cookies mom" he said. I heard his parents talking to Mac some more while Andrew patted me some more. Then they all left!

Well, that was weird. We all thought for sure they'd take one of us home; we're just too cute to resist you know.

Mac opened the gate so we could go back to the pasture to graze, but he stopped me from going. "No, you're stayin' here little guy. We got some work to do".

He took me in the barn where some other minis were kept. They were being trained how to wear bridles and bits and harnesses. He soon got me used to all that stuff, too. Well, I couldn't see why it was necessary, but I enjoyed the carrots he gave us when we did what he wanted. One day, he started walking behind us with long lines, teaching us to go and stop, and turn right and left when he said to.

It was pretty easy stuff. Then the other minis started being trained, learned to pull a cart around. It wouldn't be long before they were ready to go to their new homes.

Mac kept walking behind me with the long lines and no cart. But now he had these jingle bells with him. He shook the bells while he walked behind me with the long lines. When he stopped shaking the bells I learned that next he would pull the lines connected to my mouth. I didn't like that, so as soon as I didn't hear the bells jingle I stopped. Mac praised me and fed me a piece of carrot.

After that, he didn't have to pull the lines. Every time the bells stopped jingling, I would stop. The days passed. Finally one day, Mac hitched my harness to the cart. I could feel and hear it following me, but I could also hear Macs voice back there, so I knew it wasn't a scary monster or anything. And Mac did the same thing with the bells, so it was very familiar.

One morning Mac led me past my stall on our way to

get hitched to the cart. WHAT was that wonderful smell coming from my stall? Could it be oatmeal cookies? I wanted to stop and find out in the worst way, but Mac pulled me on past. I pranced impatiently to the cart. Let's get this lesson over with, I want my cookies!

Mac hitched me to the cart, then we trotted around the yard for a while. Then the jingling stopped. So did I. Nothing happened for a few seconds. Then the cart started jerking my harness and my mouth too. I shook my head to loosen the lines pulling on my mouth. There still was no jingling.

Just the cart jerking and shaking. I stood there awhile impatient, thinking about the treat back in my stall. One of the lines was still pulling on my mouth, so I turned my head in that direction, and took a few steps.

The line kept loose as long as I kept turning, 'til I was facing the barn. The cart was still shaking, which was really getting annoying by now. I started moving slowly towards the barn, still waiting for Mac to jingle or say SOMETHING!

When I got to the barn, there was my feed bucket with several oatmeal cookies in it sitting by the barn door.

YUM! I gobbled up the cookies, and Mac praised me the whole time. I didn't know what I did for the praise, but I loved it…and the cookies too, of course!

I enjoy a good roll after my lesson with mac

Every day Mac and I went out in the yard, me pulling, Mac jingling and sometimes shaking the cart. I knew the shaking meant to turn and go home, even without the jingle bells ringing.

I also learned if I tried to go home on my own when the cart wasn't shaking, Mac would say NO! sternly, and then pull on the lines to turn me back around.

THAT wasn't any fun, so it didn't take long for me to figure out that no jingling plus a shaking cart meant to go home, which meant yummy treats and praise.

And I learned to stand still and not move 'til the cart shook, or the jingling started. Mac would stop and talk to someone in the yard, and if I moved before he started shaking those bells, he would pull the lines quickly, with a stern NO.

NOT so much the bath he gave me afterward

All this training and remembering what I should and should not do took time, but eventually I got really good at it. One morning visitors came. It was the Andersons, with their boy Andrew. Mac brought me out pulling the cart. He got in and showed them how good I was with the jingly bells and shaking.

I could hear them talking. Everyone sounded really happy, and Andrew just smelled so GOOD! I remembered that smell, and even though I was still hitched to the cart, I went over to him and buried my nose in his pocket. YUM!! I came out chewing happily on an oatmeal cookie. They all laughed but I didn't care. I was in cookie heaven.

Mac had the boy climb into the cart with him, and showed him how to hold the bells with the reins so they would jingle, telling me to walk on, or trot when he jiggled the reins more.

I heard the boy's parents encouraging him as we circled the yard. Mac got out so Andrew could try on his own. I started out circling the yard. Andrew waved at his parents and Mac, and dropped the bells. One ear was tipped back to hear the jingle, and when it stopped, so did I.

Andrew shook the reins, saying "walk on", but I didn't move. Mac reminded Andrew I was trained to stand still when the jingling stopped. "Oops" he said, *bending to pick up the bells, and I trotted on with the jingle.*

But he must have dropped them again, because they stopped. So did I, but I was thinking 'butterfingers'. Then the cart started to jerk. It didn't feel the same as when Mac was in the cart, but I turned towards the barn anyway and headed towards it. Andrews' parents just thought he'd bent down to pick up the bells when he went out of sight. Then they and Mac

saw the loose reins at the same time and ran over just as I got to the barn. The next minutes were kinda' confusing as the adults got to me and the cart and took care of Andrew, who had had a seizure. They were talking seriously. I stood there waiting for my treat. Didn't I do it right? I saw them lift Andrew out and lay him on the grassy yard. The cart stopped shaking and I stood still. But I stomped my foot impatiently.

Hey! Where's my treat? In a few minutes I saw Andrew get up. His mom hugged him and murmured quietly to him. Then they all walked over to me. Andrew gave me a cookie. Mom gave me a cookie. Dad gave me a cookie. I looked at Mac expectantly. He laughed and gave me...a carrot. Oh well, guess I did good after all. Andrew was still pale, but he said "It worked Mom! Wait'll we get him home! Now I can ride with the other kids when they go out on their horses, yay!"

I heard Andrews' dad telling Mac he'd be over tomorrow with a trailer. "I'll have the paperwork ready for you" Mac said.

The Andersons left, Andrew waving goodbye out the car window. Mac unhitched me and put me in the barn. "Ya did real good today little guy" he said. I got a scoop of grain with another carrot chopped up in it and a big flake of hay. Mac brushed me and combed my mane and tail 'til they were silky smooth. Then he turned out the lights in the barn and left. I was too excited thinking about the new home I was going to tomorrow to sleep. So I just closed my eyes for a minute to rest them.

The crunch of tires on the gravel driveway opened my eyes. It was morning! My new owners were here! I pranced impatiently as Mac led me out. A big shiny blue trailer with a ramp going up into it was parked in the yard. The Andersons were waiting for me. "Just gotta finish filling in one thing on the little guys papers. His name." Mac said. Andrews' parents looked expectantly at their son. He walked up to Mac and very seriously took the pen from him, and wrote

'Oatmeal C. Anderson' on the line marked 'horses' name' "What's the 'C.' stand for?" Mac asked with amusement. Andrew looked up with a big grin and said "Cookie, of course!" Andrew walked me into the trailer. He gave me a cookie. Mac made sure I was tied safely, and fed me a carrot. "So long little guy" he said. "Be a good boy". Andrew and his parents got in the truck. The truck started up. "C'mon, Oatmeal, let's go home!" Andrew said.

And we did.

FROM THE AUTHOR...

I wrote this book to draw attention to the wonderful equine therapy programs that are available to help all who face tough challenges, both emotional and physical. I volunteer at one such place. It's called Veterans Serendipity Ranch. Most of the horses there have been rescued from neglectful and abusive situations.

They are rehabilitated, and given a loving home at the 'ranch' being therapy horses, for our Veterans and all those dealing with PTSD issues. For more information about Veteran Serendipity Ranch, go to their Facebook page at Veteran Serendipity Ranch, and may God richly bless you!

Patti Letts

OATMEAL C. ANDERSON

Grandma Pawleys'
Yum Yum Oatmeal Cookies

You will need 1 cup each:
brown sugar, white sugar
flour, coconut
english walnuts or almonds
melted shortening or butter
1 teaspoon ea.: vanilla, baking
powder, baking soda
1 egg
3 cups oatmeal
Powdered sugar

Cream sugars, egg, shortening (or butter), & vanilla. Stir in flour, coconut, oatmeal, nuts, baking powder & baking soda. Drop by spoonfuls on cookie sheet. Bake at 350 for 10-12 min. dust cooled cookies with powdered sugar.

YUM YUM!

Made in the USA
Lexington, KY
20 August 2017